Tiny Goat

by Iris Josiah

Published in the United Kingdom by:

Tiny Island Press
1 Bromley Lane
Chislehurst
Kent BR7 6LH, U.K

Copyright © Iris Josiah, 2012
Illustrations by Jane-Ann Cameron
Design & layout by Re-shape Invent

A CIP record of this book is available from the British Library
Printed 1 November 2012

ISBN: 978-0-9572728-2-8
Printed in the United Kingdom

Tiny Goat was a dandy little goat that lived in a dandy little house, in a little village, on Tiny Island.

Tiny Goat loved to travel and was known to everyone.

He would TRAVEL and TRAVEL and TRAVEL from village to village and town to town. NEAT and TIDY, BRIGHT and DANDY, Tiny Goat caught the attention of everyone as he travelled across Tiny Island.

Yes, everyone knew Tiny Goat and Tiny Goat knew everyone, all because of his neat and colourful appearance.

But there was a problem. For many years, many of the other animals whispered about him, all because of his dandy appearance. They WHISPERED and WHISPERED and WHISPERED.

'Oh dear, what a dandy little chap,' whispered Tiny Hen.

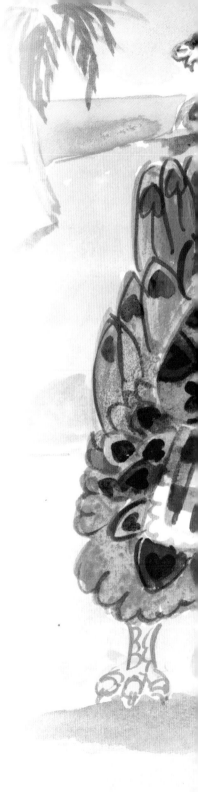

'What a jolly little fellow,' whispered Tiny Cow.

'Ummmmm,' whispered others.

Poor Tiny Goat! He knew of the whispers but did not say anything. Though, sometimes, this troubled him.

Oh yes, Tiny Goat was NEAT and TIDY, BRIGHT and SHINY; NEAT and TIDY, BRIGHT and DANDY. And Tiny Goat was always happy. He was very polite to everyone.

So happy was Tiny Goat that he would often be heard WHISTLING and WHISTLING and WHISTLING as he tidied his dandy little house and weeded his beautifully kept garden.

So polite was Tiny Goat
that he would greet and
greet everyone.

But Tiny Goat had become a little distant lately and many of his neighbours had noticed a change in him. No longer did he greet everyone. Days had passed and he had not been seen by anyone.

Soon, word spread throughout Tiny Island that Tiny Goat was missing. 'Oh, what have we done?' said everyone. 'We must stop our whispering.'

'Tiny Goat, Tiny Goat,' called his best friend Tiny Pig who had come to visit him. But Tiny Goat did not answer.

'We must go and look for him,' said the others.

So, off went Tiny Hen,
Tiny Pig, Tiny Owl,
Tiny Cow and Tiny Rabbit
to find him. But, unknown
to everyone, Tiny Goat
had not left his house
for days. He had simply
become TIRED and
TIRED and TIRED of the
whispering.

Tiny Goat had become so tired that he had distanced himself from everyone including his best friend Tiny Pig.

Soon, it was dusk and Tiny Hen, Tiny Pig, Tiny Owl, Tiny Cow and Tiny Rabbit returned to the village.

'Oh,' they cried, 'we cannot find him.'

'Oh,' cried Tiny Hen, 'what a nice, nice fellow.'

'Oh,' cried Tiny Cow, 'what a polite and helpful chap.'

And they made their way to Tiny Goat's house who overheard everything.

And, to everyone's surprise, Tiny Goat opened the door to his dandy little house looking NEAT and TIDY, BRIGHT and DANDY. And Tiny Hen, Tiny Pig, Tiny Owl, Tiny Cow and Tiny Rabbit rushed towards him. And they held and hugged and kissed him.

Soon after, news went around Tiny Island that Tiny Goat was found and everyone cried, 'what a nice, nice fellow.' And they all stopped their whispering.